Things are Looking Up, Jack

AN
ORCA
YOUNG
READER

Things are Looking Up, Jack

Dan Bar-el

ORCA BOOK PUBLISHERS

National Library of Canada Cataloguing in Publication Data
Bar-el, Dan.

Things are looking up, Jack / Dan Bar-el.

"Orca young readers."

ISBN 1-55143-278-1

I. Title.

PS8553.A76229T44 2003   jC813'.54   C2003-910878-3

PZ7.B37T44 2003

Library of Congress Catalog Card Number: 2003107506

Summary: Fantasy, parody. All around the kingdom, things are falling: Humpty Dumpty, London Bridge, the sky, even King Jack himself. What is he to do?
Teachers' guide available at www.orcabook.com

Orca Book Publishers gratefully acknowledges the support of its publishing programs provided by the following agencies: the Department of Canadian Heritage, the Canada Council for the Arts, and the British Columbia Arts Council.

Cover design by Christine Toller
Cover & interior illustrations by Kathy Boake
Printed and bound in Canada

IN CANADA	**IN THE UNITED STATES**
Orca Book Publishers	Orca Book Publishers
1030 North Park Street	PO Box 468
Victoria, BC Canada	Custer, WA USA
V8T 1C6	98240-0468

05 04 03 • 5 4 3 2 1

For Dominique, my parents Shirley & Avihu,
and sister Leora
For all their love and support.
(oh, and Monsieur Noir too)

Chapter One

Jill came tumbling after Jack, and that was when things started to go all wrong. Allow me to explain.

Jack and Jill went up a hill to fetch a pail of water. That is to say that King Jack, the twelve-year-old son of Mrs. Goose, the Queen Mother, fetched the pail of water. He did it all by himself to prove that he was not a spoiled king.

Not that he needed to prove this

because everyone in his kingdom knew that King Jack was not spoiled. Jack never wore fancy clothes or shoes. He never turned his nose up at anyone, no matter how poor or sick or different they might be. He never bossed around a single soul. King Jack was as unspoiled as the rolling countryside he ruled over.

A lot of people in Jack's kingdom would have been more than happy to fetch water for him. Not because they thought that he was too important or special for such chores. No, it was more to do with how bad Jack was at performing them. To be blunt, King Jack was clumsy. He lacked grace. Klutzy is another word that comes to mind. King Jack did not excel at many many things. He was dreadful with a bow and arrow, or with a sword. He wasn't even very good with a fork and spoon. His younger sister, Princess Jill, on the other hand, was a well-coordinated person able to jump fences with her horse, or hit bull's-eyes with an arrow. And she knew her way around eating utensils, to boot.

But Jack never ever wanted to become lazy or pampered. That is why he insisted upon fetching his own pail of water, end of discussion. Princess Jill, who *was* a bit spoiled, and would never ever do the simplest chore if it could be done by someone else, tagged along mainly to bug him.

Up the hill Jack went to fetch the water. So far, so good. But as he was about to return to the castle with the metal pail, now full of water, he fell. He didn't trip. He didn't slip. He just fell down. And Jill, who wasn't expecting this sudden change in plan, lost her balance and fell down the hill too. Thus Jill came tumbling after Jack.

"Nice going, Jack," said Jill, not really meaning it.

"Ouch," replied King Jack, rubbing his royal head. "I think I broke my crown.

Look, there's a dent in it. That's rather annoying."

"Next time, brother, let the servants fetch the water."

Jack wiped the dirt off his royal sneakers. He pushed back his mousy brown hair and puffed out his thin chest, displaying a more or less proud and noble figure. "I'm not that kind of king," he declared in a majestic voice that squeaked a little. "I want to lead by example."

Jill thought about that. "You mean you want everyone to fall down hills?"

"No, sister. I want everyone to do their fair share of work."

"You talk the talk, Jack, but you most surely do not walk the walk. At least not very well." Jill was still picking wet grass and moss from her hair. Princess Jill was one year younger than Jack, but since she considered herself better than he was at doing . . . well, anything, that made them the same age. Which was why she thought it was unfair that Jack got to be king, while she had to make do with being a princess. Teasing him about his clumsiness didn't make up for the unfairness, but it helped.

For his part, Jack smiled kindly at his frowning sister. Some days it was easier to smile than other days. On Jill's birthdays, when she received lots of presents that were exactly what she wanted (because she had her wish list posted throughout the kingdom), it was easy to smile. On days when Jill left banana skins and oil slicks all over the castle floors and declared it was the Royal Obstacle Course (which Jack failed painfully at), smiling was a little bit harder.

Overall, Jack was an optimist. He believed that everything would always turn out for the best. Whatever he lacked in skills or coordination didn't really matter because he made up for his failings with smiles. Jack's optimism was like a metal shield protecting him from adversity. Jack's sister, however, was like a steady drizzle of rain that could cause his shield to rust.

"Ha, ha, ha," said Jill.

"What's so funny? Do I have mud on my nose?"

"I'm not laughing, Jack. I'm reading. Look at the hedge behind you. It's been pruned to read 'HA HA HA.' Shrubs should be shaped into birds or squirrels. I hate this modern stuff!"

"I'll have a talk with the royal gardener," said Jack. He reached for his sister's hand to help her up when suddenly, from a little way up the road, they heard a CRASH, then a SPLAT, followed by a "Yuck!"

Humpty Dumpty had fallen off the wall. Jack let go of Jill's hand and rushed to the side of his injured knight. Jill landed back onto the soggy dirty ground and grumbled something un-princess-like.

"Are you all right, Sir Dumpty?" asked the concerned King Jack.

The often jovial, and usually oval,

knight tried to get up onto his legs in order to bow before his lord. His efforts were less than successful and he collapsed in his own yolk. This time, King Jack had nothing to do with it.

Poor Sir Dumpty was cracked, his thoughts were scrambled, his nerves were fried and if there was a sunny side to his mood, it wasn't presently facing up. "Apparently I am not all right, your Majesty. This is dreadfully embarrassing. I seem to have egg all over my face."

"There, there," said Jack, patting Humpty's sticky hand.

On a good day, Humpty Dumpty would have made a much different impression. He was, after all, a proud egg who had worked his way up to become head of the castle guard. This was quite an achievement considering all the snide comments he had to put up with. Some were jealous of his success. They protested that although he may appear brave, beneath his shell beat the heart of a chicken. This was unfair. Those who really knew him thought Sir Humpty was a loyal dependable knight who would always be there in your time of need. Jack thought quite highly of him, sometimes talking to Humpty Dumpty as if he was the father that Jack never had a chance to know.

"I don't understand it," the broken egg cried. "I was just sitting here on top of the wall as I usually do in the mornings, knitting egg cozies. The sun was shining. The birds were chirping and looking at me with their usual, curious expression. There wasn't any wind. The earth didn't shake. One second I was up there and the next second I was down here. I don't understand how this happened. I've never fallen before."

"He was probably just following your example, Jack," said Jill with a smirk.

Jack decided to royally ignore his sister. "This is quite a coincidence. I, myself, have also just fallen down for no apparent reason," said Jack with complete sincerity.

Sir Humpty looked up at Jack and raised one eyebrow in a most incredulous fashion. Although he loved Jack like his own son, had sworn to protect him with his own life, had watched Jack grow up from a swaddled infant into the fine, young man he was becoming, Sir Humpty took no comfort in Jack's observation. Jack falling down was a regular occurrence. Jack *not* falling down would be more cause for alarm. "Amazing coincidence," said Humpty Dumpty, not really meaning it.

"Husha, husha, we all fall down," said Jill.

There was a brief silence when both Sir Humpty and Jack stared at Jill as if she had just said something very strange, which, as a matter of fact, she had.

"What?" Jill asked innocently.

"Perhaps the princess is not feeling up to snuff," offered Humpty Dumpty politely.

"Husha, husha, Jill?" added Jack,

"what are you babbling about?"

"I'm not making it up! Look, someone painted that on the wall."

Sure enough, just to the right of them, along the gray stone wall was written, "HUSHA, HUSHA, WE ALL FALL DOWN," in white paint.

"And the paint is still wet," said Jack, after he touched it. "Whoever did this was here not too long ago."

"Vandals! Hoodlums!" shouted Sir Humpty, who did not approve of damage to public property, especially his favorite sitting spot. "I will catch them, I swear it!"

"Perhaps," agreed King Jack. "But for now, you need attention. Shall I send my horses and men, Sir Dumpty? Perhaps they could put you together again."

"Oh no, don't bother," sighed Sir Dumpty as he imagined all the snickers he would have to endure from his junior guards. "A spatula would be nice, though. And some duct tape."

Chapter Two

After Jack found a royal guard to assist Sir Humpty, he and Jill continued their walk back to the castle. As usual, they took a shortcut through the royal park, a densely forested area with winding paths of cobblestones. As usual, they walked past various royal subjects who all happily bowed or curtsied before them. What was not usual was that King Jack did not wave back.

Ordinarily, Jack was a very friendly king. At Jack's school, where everyone was named Jack, he was voted as the Jack most likely to be liked. Other Jacks were voted most nimble or quick or most likely to live in a box, but King Jack was just plain nice.

People said that Jack was as kind-hearted as his father, who too was called Jack. Sadly, neither Jack nor Jill got to know him because he died when they were very young. How he died remains a mystery. Some say a monster was involved. Others say it was a nasty giant. What *is* known (and never talked about anymore), was that he was crushed, flat as a pancake, thin as a flag flapping in the wind.

Nonetheless, Jack relished hearing those comparisons with his father. In a small way, it made him feel that they were connected. Jack liked to think that somewhere his dad was smiling whenever a likeness was being made between father and son. But this worked both ways because aside from being kind-hearted, people remembered Jack Senior as being a strong, spry, able-bodied, natural born leader. Jack could just blush every time he did something awkward.

Jack imagined his dad was wincing with embarrassment every time Jack dropped a plate, walked into a door or slipped on a stair. Why couldn't he be more coordinated and spirited like his sister Jill?

Tripping down a perfectly ordinary hill! Jack scolded himself silently. And yet I'm sure I didn't trip. I just fell. And so did Sir Humpty, and *he* isn't clumsy.

Those were the deep thoughts pre-occupying Jack as he walked, thoughts that left a concerned look on his face. His eyebrows were bunched together like furry accordions, and his lips were squeezed even tighter. Jill, who was walking directly behind her big brother, had exactly the same expression, but she also had her thumbs in her ears and was wiggling her fingers. At Jill's school, where everyone was named Jill, she was voted as the Jill most likely to get locked up in a dungeon or fed to a dragon.

Brother and sister meandered their way through the tree-lined path when they heard a gentle voice singing a soft lullaby. Around the corner, they found an old woman easing her grandchild to sleep. "Rock a bye baby in the tree top. When the wind blows, the cradle will rock."

Jill smiled at her brother and even he could not help but smile back. They knew this rhyme well, having heard it many times as children themselves. "When the bough breaks, the cradle will fly," they both sang. "And up will go baby into the sky."

Then suddenly, there was a SNAP, then a "GASP," followed by a FLOP! Snap went the tree branch. "Gasp" went the grandmother in horror. Flop went

the baby into Jill's hands, who had just barely made it in time to catch her. Jill put the baby into the grand-mother's outstretched arms.

"The bough broke and . . . and the baby fell . . . with, with the cradle . . . and all!" stammered the terribly shaken woman. "Poor, little thing!"

"There, there," said King Jack. "I'm sure she will be quite fine."

"Thank you, your Majesty. I don't understand it, though. I've been rocking this baby everyday at the same tree since she was two weeks old. There has never been a problem before."

"Your grandchild hasn't put on a lot of weight lately, has she?"

"Sister!" yelled a flustered King Jack to Princess Jill.

Jill just shrugged her shoulders innocently.

"What my sister meant," explained Jack as he smiled nervously, "is that the world is vast and unexplainable. . . and . . . And within such a big . . .

huge . . . world . . . uh, all things are possible?"

"Are you calling my grandchild fat?" the old woman asked in a low growl. She began to swing her handbag like a mace. King or no king, this was her grandchild being insulted.

"No, not at all, Madam! I mean nothing of the sort!" Jack quickly decided to cut his losses and avoid major injury. "We really must be off now. Good day." Jack pulled his sister away before she had any other thoughts to share with the potentially dangerous grandmother, and they both ran.

They ran until they were at a safe distance and soon approaching the castle gate. Jill, who did not like being dragged around by her big brother, yanked her arm away with a "hmmph."

"Don't get all pouty, Jill. That was a rude thing to say about her baby. Can't you ever be civil?"

"I didn't say it, Jack. I admit that I might have thought it, but the words did not come from my mouth."

"There was no one else there, sister! I didn't say it, the grandmother didn't say it and the baby certainly didn't say it. So?"

Jill looked at her brother very seriously. "There was someone else. At least, I think there was. Just as you pulled me away, I saw a person hiding in the trees."

"Oh?" replied Jack, not sure if Jill was trying to fool him or not. "What did this person look like?"

"That's the weird thing. I couldn't tell you. It's like trying to describe someone that has no details, no features; someone that is completely unremarkable in every way."

"Sure. That sounds believable," said Jack, not really meaning it.

Jill didn't care what her brother believed. She saw what she saw, and so what anyway; it was lunch time. She set her mind upon the afternoon luncheon that her mother was hosting. Nothing made Princess Jill happier than to insult guests, boss around the servants and eat little tidbits with toothpicks. They were going to be late, but Jack still didn't move.

"Something is wrong in the kingdom, wouldn't you agree?"

"No, because I don't care. I'm hungry," Jill insisted. Her stomach agreed with *her*.

"It's odd," said Jack, not paying attention either to his sister or her stomach.

Jill sighed and prepared herself for a Crackpot-Jackpot speech. That was when her brother would form a crazy theory based on nothing much, and that was usually preceded by Jack saying, "It's odd."

"Quite odd," repeated Jack.

"Big sigh," repeated Jill, sighing loudly.

"Think about it, sister. I fell down a gently sloped hill for no apparent reason. I didn't trip. I wasn't pushed.

I just fell. Then you fell after me. And shortly after that, Sir Dumpty falls off the same wall he's been sitting on for years. Lastly, a baby's cradle falls to the ground after weeks of problem-free rocking."

Jill might have added something about the unremarkable stranger hiding in the trees, but it wouldn't have made any difference. Whatever Jack's hunch was, it was bound to be goofy.

"Perhaps it has something to do with it being Tuesday. I've never trusted Tuesdays, sister. They're sneaky. Anyway, something is amiss, I tell you."

"Too strange," agreed Jill, not really meaning it.

"I see no rhyme or reason for all this painful falling," Jack declared.

"All right, Jack!" Jill said. "Now, can we eat, please?"

Chapter Three

Mother Goose, the queen mother of King Jack and Princess Jill, was hosting her lunch party with her usual charm and style. She was not a real goose, you understand. She was simply goose-like. Her laugh, although quite spirited, sounded very much like a quack. When she blew her nose, the honk that came out was enough to bring game wardens running from miles away. When she walked, and there is no nice way of putting this, she waddled. But none of this made her any less lovable to her royal subjects, who all called her Mother Goose out of true affection.

Currently, Mother Goose was listening to a short young man with a purple thumb, while sneaking peeks at the clock hanging at the back of the castle's great hall. Her dear children were late, and she was not impressed.

Quack-quack-quack-quack! "Oh, Mr. Horner, you tell the most hilarious stories. Imagine finding a plum in your mincemeat pie, with your thumb of all things! Is that why it's purple?"

"No, Mum, I hit it with a hammer by accident this morning. Very painful."

"How delightful," replied Mother Goose, who had stopped listening because she was distracted by the entrance of Jack and Jill. She waved in their direction.

But Jack and Jill were not allowed to enter the great hall until Reginald, the castle butler, checked his clipboard that held the official guest list.

"Name, please?"

"Oh, come on Reginald," hissed an exasperated Jill, "You know who we are."

Reginald took his job very seriously. Some might say that he took his job too seriously. There were always gate crashers at the Queen Mother's parties and he was determined to sniff them out.

"I will know who you are when you tell me your names."

"I am King Jack," said King Jack calmly, "and this is Princess Jill."

"Ah, yes," said Reginald, who was happy to finally get some cooperation. He then spent a good minute running his finger down the list until he found what he was looking for. "One Jack, King and one Jill, Princess."

"No, no, Reginald. I am King Jack,

as in His Royal Majesty of this castle."

"And I am Princess Jill, as in your employer, capable of having your head if I miss out on the hors d'oeuvres."

"I always enter last names first and first names last," explained Reginald, as if he was talking to two very slow-thinking gerbils. "For example, one Horner, Jack is here, as is one Spratt, Jack."

"Where have you two ill-mannered children been?" scolded Mother Goose, waddling towards them through the crowds. "The party started well over an hour ago."

"Sorry, Mother," said Jack after giving her a peck on the cheek. "We made some very odd discoveries this morning."

"Yes," said Jill, while searching the room for servants holding plates full of cocktail wieners. "For one thing, Jack is incapable of walking and carrying water at the same time. Secondly, the babies in our kingdom are eating much too much. And thirdly, poor Sir Humpty is a hollow shell of his former self."

The Queen Mother stared blankly at her daughter for a very long time until she finally turned to Jack and asked, "Whatever is your sister talking about?"

Jack had no time to answer because at that moment there was a CRASH! Then a *GASP!* Followed by a *CLUCK*. The crash came from a servant tripping and dropping the last plate of cocktail wieners. The gasp came from either the shocked guests or the very hungry Jill. The *cluck* came from a small chicken presently running around the great hall. This was not a chicken-like person, but an actual chicken, and this chicken was not very calm.

"The sky is falling! The sky is falling!"

"Reginald, who is that rather excited fowl?" asked Jack.

Reginald studied the list of invited guests.

"I presume that must be one Little, Chicken, your Majesty."

"Obviously!" shouted Jack, who was having just about enough of the impertinent Reginald, "I can see for myself that it is a small chicken. I asked for its name!"

"But your Highness," insisted Reginald, "the little chicken's name is Chicken Little."

"How amusing," declared Jill. "I think everyone should be named so aptly. You, dear brother, would be called not simply King Jack, but rather Clumsy King Jack."

"And you, dear sister, would be more suited to a name like Forever-in-the-Dungeon Jill."

Jill darted over to the finger food table. Reginald darted back to his post.

"Mr. Little," called Jack, "Please come over here."

The small fowl, otherwise known as Chicken Little, rushed over to the king. "Your Majesty, the sky is falling as we speak!"

"That is the most absurd thing I've ever heard." *Honk*! Mother Goose was allergic to chicken feathers.

"Ordinarily I would agree, Mother, but after what Jill and I saw this morning, it could be plausible. Tell us more, Chicken."

"Well, your Majesty, I was coming back from London when suddenly I felt what I thought was a drop of water. But how could it be raining when the sky was mainly blue? Upon closer inspection, the raindrop was in actual fact a bee. It just fell."

"Goodness," said Jack.

Honk! sneezed his mother.

"But that's not all. Soon the ground was covered with thousands and thousands of flies, bees, wasps, and hornets who were all as surprised as I. But after the insects came the birds: crows and seagulls and pigeons and at least one pelican that I know of."

"Goodness," repeated Jack.

Honk! Honk! sneezed Mother Goose.

"But that's not all. After the birds

came the clouds and they landed with a horrible crash!"

"Soft fluffy clouds thudding to the ground?" asked Jack.

"Not the actual clouds," explained Chicken Little, "but all those magical castles on them. One poor giant was rather upset. He just got rid of his beanstalk problem when his home suddenly smashes to pieces."

King Jack had heard enough. Something was wrong, and he was going to get to the bottom of it. "Where exactly did you see this happen?"

"On the road to London, your Majesty," Chicken Little replied. "On the other side of the river, near Peter Pumpkin Eater's place."

Jack turned to his mother and bowed. "I'm sorry but I must go immediately."

"*You* are not going anywhere! You are not the king. You are, in fact, one Big, Chicken!" It was Reginald and he was looking at Jack as if he had uncovered a spy.

"Reginald!" shouted Mother Goose. "That is my son you insult. You dare call the king a coward?"

"No, no, your Majesty. What I mean is that his name is actually Chicken Big."

"Who on earth told you such a thing, Reginald?" asked Jack.

"Why that man over . . . uh . . . where did he go?" Reginald stretched his neck in all directions searching above the crowd. "He disappeared! I'm sorry, your Highness. I got carried away. He was very convincing!"

"A man told you that I was Chicken Big so that you would then reverse the name and call me a big chicken? Describe this man, Reginald." Jack insisted.

"Well, at least I think he was a man. He was . . . well, he looked like . . . he seemed to be . . . It's strange, but I can't really think of anything that was remarkable about him."

"Hmm. I guess that Jill wasn't lying, after all," thought Jack. "Who *is* this man and what does he want from me? And why bother me now, with all the problems in the kingdom?" Again, Jack bowed to his take his leave.

"But Jack," cried his mother. "Why can't you let our good knights take care of it? Surely Sir Humpty could be consulted."

"Sir Humpty has been injured, and besides, I'm not that kind of king, mother. I lead by example. If something is threatening the safety of our land, it is my responsibility to stop it."

Jack turned towards the door with a regal flourish. So determined was he that he didn't even notice the plate and goblet that he knocked from the two startled guests standing beside him. Jack left the great hall with his head held high . . . and a small juice stain on his shirt sleeve.

"What an impressive king," remarked Chicken Little who was genuinely impressed.

Honk! added Mother Goose.

A howl of pain came from the direction of the food table. Princess Jill was standing beside Georgie Porgie, who was hopping up and down on one leg, while cradling his other foot in his hands. Mother Goose was not thrilled about how this party was turning out.

"Mr. Porgie, pray tell what causes you to caterwaul like such?" she asked, not too kindly.

"She . . . your daughter . . . she . . . owwww! Boo-hoo-hoo!" Georgie Porgie continued to cry.

"Oh, for goodness sake, what is his problem?"

"I kicked him, Mother," explained Jill. "In the shin," she added.

"Whatever for?"

"He kissed me."

"But that's what he does. Georgie Porgie kisses all the girls."

"Well, he isn't kissing this one," said Princess Jill with her arms crossed.

Mother Goose was getting a headache. She took a deep breath and turned to the sniveling young man. "There, there, Mr. Porgie. Feeling a little better then?"

"Yes, Mum, a little," he pouted.

"Why don't you go to the dessert table and help yourself to a generous portion of pudding and pie?"

"Pie?" said Georgie, his tears drying immediately. "Mmmmmm." Georgie Porgie was feeling much better as he left them.

"Where's Jack, Mother?" asked Jill.

"Your brother has rudely taken off towards London concerning falling clouds or some such rubbish. It's a wonder how I manage all alone with the two of you. If you're not playing hopscotch on the castle roof or picking on someone twice as big as you, well, then it's your brother tripping over his shadow or trying to save the kingdom. Imagine leaving one of my luncheons so early. At least you're here to comfort me, my dear, dear Jill. Jill?"

But Jill was not there either, for she was off to find Jack. Jack trying to save the kingdom, she thought. Ha! Not likely. He'll need me for sure.

As Jill left the great hall, three game wardens came in. They all held large nets and were looking suspiciously at Mother Goose.

"Oh, wonderful," said Mother Goose, not really meaning it.

Chapter Four

Impressive King Jack gallantly rode his galloping steed towards London. Or to be truly honest, Jack rode a short trotting pony. As you may have already guessed, Jack had not earned a reputation for horsemanship. He tried riding a horse once, and once was all he needed. If there were two things that Jack quickly learned about horses it was that they liked sugar cubes and they liked to throw him into ditches. Jack suspected that sugar cubes came a distant second to king-tossing for a horse. A pony was much better suited for Jack's taste.

Since traveling by a slow, plodding animal makes a journey somewhat longer, Jack had more time to reflect upon the possible danger that awaited him and how ill-prepared he was to meet that danger. Running through every possible worst-case scenario, Jack was able to envision many horrible ways he could end up getting hurt.

If earthquakes were behind all this, then the road could split open and Jack might fall into a deep chasm. Since he was not a strong climber, he might fall and break one or all of his bones.

If a dragon was behind all this (and dragons do not have a great reputation in Jack's kingdom), he would have to confront it, and since he was not good with sword or ax or any weapon really, it would likely mean him getting charbroiled, trampled upon or possibly ripped apart. Again, lots of pain involved.

If it was a — Jack stopped himself mid-thought. Hold on there, he told himself. This is not the kind of thinking an optimist indulges in. Something will turn up, no matter what the problem is, so don't worry about it now.

"Hello, Jack. Thought you could go on an adventure without me, did you?"

Jack looked all around to find where the mysterious voice came from. He looked left and right, forwards and backwards and couldn't see a thing. Finally, he glanced skywards to find Jill riding a big white stallion at a much faster speed than his small pony. He had to look up because at that moment, Jill's horse was jumping over him and his small pony.

"Jill, no one said you could come along. Giants are falling from clouds. This could be dangerous."

"I don't care if it's dangerous."

"Well, as your big brother, I have to be concerned for your safety," Jack

said as Jill made her horse jump over him again. "And stop doing that!"

"Not until you agree to let me come with you," replied Jill defiantly.

"No!"

"Come on, Jack. You may be older but, let's face it, you could use some help from me. I'm more skilled than you in a lot of ways that might come in handy."

"Ha!" exclaimed King Jack, "Name one!"

"Horse riding," said Jill without a pause.

Jack could hardly disagree since Jill was having this whole conversation while riding backwards on her horse. Her feet were extended and her head was lying back against her horse's neck like it was a pillow.

"Name another!" Jack dared his sister, although he regretted it as soon as he said it.

"Jousting, fencing, archery, crossbow, longbow, spear throwing, running, climbing, jumping, swimming, skating, and long-distance spitting. Face it, Jack, you could use me."

Jill had a point and Jack knew that a smart king does not ignore good advice. Jack was actually proud of his sister's abilities. Not that he was going to admit it to her because Jack knew that a smart big brother does not let his little sister get a swelled head.

"I still must say no, Jill."

"Come on, Jack, I'm bored! You're the one who got to be King."

"I'm older than you."

"Just barely. It's not fair! You get to make speeches and greet important visitors and attend ribbon-cutting ceremonies. I'm just 'the princess.' I'm expected to curtsy and smile and sew pillow slips."

"None of which you have ever done," Jack threw in quickly. "You're hotheaded and stubborn. You've always done whatever you wanted. As if you would ever attend a ribbon-cutting ceremony. You're the lucky one, Jill. You get to climb trees and wrestle with wild animals and shoot crossbows. I wish I had the time to do that!"

"Ha!" yelled Jill as she stood up on her galloping horse. "As if you could ever do any of those things! You couldn't climb a tree if you had a hundred squirrels glued to your arms and legs! You may be a nice guy like everyone says father was, but no one in their right mind would expect you to save the day like he would have."

"Well, I wish they would!" shouted Jack, nearly in tears.

Jill said nothing. She could see that she touched a nerve with her brother. Even though she was as mad at him as he was mad at her, she never meant to really hurt him.

"I know what everyone thinks about me, Jill. I know I'm a klutz and not a big risk taker. You may be bored, but I'm just boring. Maybe you *should* be in charge. You're the brave one."

"But I don't know how to talk to people like you do, Jack. You make everyone feel important and good about themselves."

Brother and sister stared at each other in amazement. It had been a very long time since either of them had anything nice to say to each other. It felt a bit strange, and even more so for Jill, who rarely had anything nice to say to anyone. King Jack needed to make a decision. He could go it alone and take a big chance that he would be able to save the kingdom from whatever was threatening it, or he could use his sister's help and share some of the glory.

"Fine, you can come," he said, "but please try to control your impulsive nature."

"I promise," replied Jill, not really meaning it. "Now, if we really want to get to the bottom of this problem, we could get there a lot faster on my horse. Jump on, Jack."

"No, I really don't . . . " Jack got out

before his sister pulled him off his pony onto the back of her moving stallion. The rest of his sentence sounded more like: "Whoa! Whoa! Ahhhhh, oh my, oh, oh my!"

"Hang on, Jack!" yelled Jill as she got the horse to pick up speed.

Jill had nothing to worry about in the hanging-on department. Bouncing King Jack was hanging on for his dear life.

Chapter Five

The sign said, "London Bridge — Straight Ahead." The sign stated the obvious to Jack and Jill because they had already seen the large structure from quite a distance away. London Bridge was a landmark in the kingdom. And yet, although it was a majestic bridge, well-proportioned and made of large blocks of granite, tourists were generally disappointed. They were expecting to see the other London Bridge. You know, the *famous* one. This London Bridge was really just a bridge that took you on the road to London and it didn't have a gift shop anywhere near it.

As Jack and Jill approached the river, they found themselves coming closer to an armored man with a loud whistle clamped between his teeth. He was a traffic-knight. "Tweet!" went his whistle, which caused the visor of his helmet to bang shut. "Halt!" yelled his voice, somewhere from within the helmet. Jill pulled her horse to a stop.

"What is it, good yeoman?" asked Jack.

The traffic-knight pushed his visor up again. "I'm sorry, your Highness, but I cannot permit you to cross the bridge at this time!"

"And why in goodness sake not, you loud, unpleasant man?" Jill growled.

"Because presently, London Bridge is falling down!"

"Falling down?" asked Jack.

"Falling down," repeated the guard, nodding his head gravely, causing his visor to slip down again.

"But I must get across the river," implored King Jack.

Up went the visor immediately. "You don't want to do that, your Majesty! There are strange things going on over there! I've heard rumors that the earth has split open! It's swallowing innocent people! The horror!" shouted the traffic-knight. "The horror!" His last shout caused his visor to slam shut again.

Jill looked at the river. It was wide and rough and not one that even she would try to swim across. "Don't worry," said Jack, sensing her frustration, "something will come up. It always does."

"Honestly, Jack, you can be so annoying with your unshakeable faith that something will always come up, even when it's perfectly obvious that nothing will."

"I can help you get across the river."

"There we go," said Jack cheerfully, "What did I tell you? Now, who just made that kind offer?"

"I did."

Jack and his sister leaned over to one side of the horse and looked down upon a head full of golden curls.

"Goldilocks?" asked Jack.

The head bent upwards to reveal a cheerful face and a cheerful smile that tugged melodically at King Jack's heartstrings. Somewhere, at least in Jack's mind, violins were playing accompaniment. "No. Miss Bo Peep, actually," said the cheerful face.

Jack took himself gracefully off the horse in one deft swoop. Or to be truly honest, Jack slid off the horse's rump and landed on his own rump. But to his credit, he did get back onto his feet without looking too silly.

Before him stood a young lady wearing an outrageously frilly dress complete with frilly handbag. Whereas other people, like Jill for instance, might have thought the costume to be a bit excessive for casual wear, Jack had only eyes for the young lady's cheerful face.

"My apologies, Miss Peep," Jack bowed, "Your resemblance to Goldilocks is uncanny."

"Yes, I get that a lot. I suppose I could have been called Goldilocks myself if it wasn't for all those sheep following me."

Jill scanned the area, which contained neither sheep nor anything remotely resembling sheep. She was beginning to wonder if Miss Bo Peep was quite right in the head. "What sheep?" asked Jill indelicately. "There are no sheep."

"That's because I lost them," Bo Peep explained simply.

"How sad," said Jack, who was looking a bit goofy as he stared at her.

"Usually I have dozens and dozens of sheep all over the place," Bo Peep continued. "I know all of them by name. There's Maisy and Daisy and

Buttercup and Lola. There's Veronica and Betty and . . ."

"Yes?" asked Jack encouragingly.

"What's the use in remembering their names if I can't remember what I did with them?"

Bo Peep's despairing expression made Jack melt.

"There, there, Miss Peep," said Jack. An icky silence followed as Jack and Bo Peep stared deeply into one another's eyes.

"Anyway," said Jill loudly, "you said you could get us across the river. How?"

"There's a boat just downstream a ways. It's hidden under a pile of straw and twigs."

"If the boat is hidden, how would you ever have known it was under the straw and twigs?" asked Jill, who didn't have nearly as much faith in Bo Peep as her brother did.

Bo Peep smiled brightly. "I didn't know about the boat until the wolf told me."

"The wolf?" asked Jack and Jill at the same time.

"Why yes, the wolf! He mentioned the boat when I passed him on the road on the other side of the river. I was searching for my flock and he suggested I look there. But to tell you the truth I don't think it was a real wolf. There was something about him that made me think it was a person disguised as a wolf. Hmm, what was it?"

"Perhaps he didn't sound mean enough," offered Jack, helpfully.

"Oh no, he sounded mean. Even scary. Although a bit out of breath. No, it was something else. Now I remember! It was the zipper running up the back of his fur."

Had there been a wall anywhere nearby, Jill would probably have been banging her head against it by now. "Yes, I suppose the zipper would have tipped you off."

"How observant you are, Miss Peep," gushed Jack.

"And how kind you are, your Majesty, to compliment me so," Bo Peep replied.

"And how humble you show yourself to be when such a small compliment can mean so much," continued Jack, causing another icky silence between the two.

"Anyway!" said Jill even more loudly. "How about if you take us to this boat?"

"Very well. It's this way."

"Miss Peep," said Jack, offering his arm. "I would be honored."

"Please, call me Bo, your Majesty."

"Oh, Bo," sighed Jack as they walked towards the riverbank.

"Oh, brother," sighed Jill as she rolled her eyes.

Chapter Six

Jack and Jill and little Bo Peep walked along the riverbank in search of the hidden boat. Jill walked behind the other two with her index fingers in her ears. She was not making a rude gesture at her brother this time. She was just trying to shut out little Bo Peep's voice.

"And then there are Jody and Cody. They're twins. And then there are Bobby and Toby and Leonard and Chuck who are all part of the same family. And then there are Wee Wooly and Little Baa."

"Miss Peep . . . I mean Bo, I could listen to you recite your sheep's names forever," said Jack, "and I promise you, that as soon as I find out what is making everything in my kingdom fall down, I will help you to find your lost flock."

"Thank you, your Majesty . . . I mean Jack. I see now why you are so well liked. Even the wolf said you were nice. Although he didn't say it in a very pleasant way."

The wolf knew me? thought Jack. But before he could ask Bo Peep another question, she was running ahead.

"Look! There it is!"

Little Bo Peep pointed to a rocky nook that held a boat, half-hidden beneath twigs and straw. It was moored to a tree stump. And it would have been completely hidden except that presently two pigs were grabbing the twigs and straw and stacking them into two separate piles. Yes, these were actual pigs and not pig-like people, although these pigs did walk on two legs and wear overalls. Such was the strangeness of living in King Jack's kingdom.

"Hello there," called Jack cheerfully as they approached the boat. The pigs stopped dead in their tracks, grabbed their pile of straw or twigs, and ran away as fast as they could. In the distance, Jack could see a third pig hauling bricks that must have come from what was left of the fallen bridge.

"What's their problem?" remarked Jill, "You'd think *they* had seen the wolf."

Together, they uncovered the boat. It was a typical boat and yet it wasn't. It was twice as large as a rowboat but much smaller than a sailing ship. It didn't have a rudder but it did have a shiny metal object where a rudder would have been. The strangest thing was that a small wheel stuck out of a box near the front of the boat.

Little Bo Peep read out loud what was written on the side of it: "THIS IS THE BOAT THAT JACK BUILT."

"I certainly didn't build it," said Jack, "but I suppose it could have been one of the other Jacks in the area. There are a lot of us."

"There are no oars!" yelled Jill, throwing her arms up in the air. "There are no oars or sails! How are we supposed to get this boat across the river?"

"Don't worry. Something will come up. It always does," said Jack and Bo Peep at the same time. This caused both of them to laugh and blush. Jill just knew that another icky silence was on the way.

In order to kill time during the icky silence, Jill fiddled about the boat until she came to the box with the wheel sticking out of it. Beside the wheel was what looked like a keyhole with a key in it. This was strange, because there was no door attached to the box. Jill turned the key anyway.

"Brrrrrrrrum-brum-brum-brum" came a roar from the back of the boat. The boat itself started to shake, and Jack, who wasn't the most balanced person to begin with, fell into the arms of Bo Peep. Bo Peep just plain fell. As strange as it all was, Jill gathered that the noise probably had something to do with making the boat move. She also noticed that the small wheel sticking out of the box was turning a little in one direction, and then turning a little in the other direction, and that the boat was always turning in the same direction as the wheel. Jill had an idea.

"I think I know how to steer the boat!" she yelled over the noise. Jack and Bo Peep were not so interested because they were much too busy falling down each time the boat shifted direction. Jill removed the rope that moored the boat to the tree stump. Then she spun the wheel, which caused the boat to turn away from the shore. It was now facing the other side of the river. Good, but how was she to make it go there?

Taking advantage of the boat no longer turning, Jack stood up to see what Jill was doing. Steadily, he worked his way forward until he was beside Jill and the box with the wheel. "How goes it?" he yelled to his sister, trying to act casual and confident in front of Bo Peep.

"It doesn't go!" yelled Jill back. "That's the problem. I can steer it but I can't make it move ahead!"

"I'm sure we can find something." Jack looked at the box. Besides the key and keyhole, there were other button-shaped objects and other glass covered objects, none of which Jack had any clue about. This did not prevent Jack from fiddling with them.

"Careful, Jack!" yelled Jill.

"Not to worry!" yelled Jack back to his sister while turning around to give a brave smile for Bo Peep's sake. This meant that Jack had to lean one elbow against the box and in doing so, pushed against the only sliding object on the box. The object slid forwards. Then the boat suddenly jerked forwards. Jack, however, found himself not moving forwards but actually moving backwards and eventually overboard into the river.

Splash!

"Help!" sputtered brave King Jack.

After Jill and Bo Peep pulled Jack back into the boat, Jill, who now knew how to make the boat move, continued driving it towards the other side of the river. Meanwhile, Bo Peep found an old blanket tucked under one of the benches and wrapped it around Jack to help him warm up. Jack, for the most part, just sat there and shivered. Sitting while you are cold, wet and shivering is not pleasant, but it does allow you to do other things like fidget, and fidget is what Jack did. He rubbed his hands together. He rubbed them against his legs. He rubbed them against the wood bench he was sitting on. Then, he felt a note. Allow me to explain.

Some people seem to enjoy writing so much that they will write even if they do not have pen or paper. These people are responsible for carving up perfectly good tree trunks and desk tops with mysterious messages like, "K.J. loves B.P" or other such nonsense. As Jack was running his fingers along the bench, he came across a note carved into the wood. It said: "YOU ARE GETTING WARMER, JACK."

"Hardly," thought Jack, who was still very wet and very cold. But when he looked closer, he saw an outline around the message that appeared to be moveable. By pushing against it, the wood piece slid away from the bench and revealed a secret drawer.

"Th - th- that's interesting," stuttered shivering Jack.

Inside the small compartment was stuffed a thin scroll. Jack pried it out and unrolled it. The scroll was a map. On the map were marked many landmarks and all of them were curious because they were not your usual map landmarks. Jack could see a tiny picture depicting London Bridge, but on this map it was broken. He could see a patch of land with lots of birds, bugs and one giant spread upon the ground. He could even see a small picture of Sir Humpty Dumpty smashed to bits beside the wall he usually sat upon.

How odd. It was as if the map was made to show what was going to happen.

This boat could well belong to someone connected to all the strange things going on, thought Jack to himself.

This was exciting news indeed, and perhaps something to make him look good in Bo Peep's eyes after his rather graceless fall in the river.

Jack stood up proudly to declare he had exciting news. Unfortunately, it was at the exact same time that Jill reached the other side of the river. She pulled the sliding object back, and the boat quickly slowed to a stop. Jack continued moving forwards as if the boat was still moving forwards. He stopped when he reached the front of the boat.

Splash!

The exciting news would have to wait until Jill and Bo Peep pulled Jack out of the river again.

Chapter Seven

The map was soggy but not damaged, and that went double for Jack. He, along with Jill and Bo Peep, studied the map as they made their way back towards the road to London.

"Look here, Jack." Jill pointed to a spot. "It says, 'Peter Pumpkin Eater's place.' Didn't you say that Chicken Little thought the sky was falling near there?"

"That's right," agreed Jack. "I think it would be reasonable for us to continue our investigation at Mr. Pumpkin Eater's residence." Jill and Bo Peep nodded their approval.

Despite the reason behind their journey, the day itself was actually quite pleasant. The meadows were dotted with the reds and yellows of hundreds of wild flowers in full blossom. The sun shone hot and bright, but a small breeze kept the three travelers comfortably cool.

"Do you like being a king?" asked Bo Peep suddenly, when Jill had gone up ahead.

No one had ever asked Jack that question before. *Did* he like being a king? He didn't really have a say in it. One morning his mother announced that she didn't want to run the kingdom anymore because she was devoting her time to writing nursery rhymes (and hosting the odd luncheon here and there). Jack, she decided, was eleven and quite capable of running the kingdom's affairs as his father had done prior.

"I don't know," Jack replied finally. "I'm not sure I'm very good at it yet. It's only been a year. I know people like me and all, but I'm not sure they would depend upon me. I'm not exactly hero material; you may have noticed. My father was a real king. I think everyone still sees me as just a small boy."

"Tell me about it," agreed Bo Peep. "In my neck of the woods, I'm still known as 'Little' Bo Peep. I'm the same age as you and almost as tall. I suppose when I'm twenty-five, they'll still be calling me 'Little.'"

Jack and Bo Peep shared a laugh that expressed entirely that they understood each other.

"I have to admit that being King Jack has been a lot better than when I was plain old Jack. Everyone used to ignore me. It was like I was invisible.

Then I started tripping and falling all the time and people would call me Clumsy Jack behind my back. That was even worse. Whenever I did anything stupid I wished I *was* invisible."

"Names are useful," said little Bo Peep, "but they don't tell you the whole story."

Jack thought about what Bo Peep had said as they made an effort to catch up with Jill. This was not as easy as it sounds. As they got closer to their destination, something was changing, and it was affecting their progress. Even though the walk was not really very far, it seemed to be taking forever. They were not tired, but Jack, Jill and Bo Peep were acting as if they were exhausted. Each step required more effort than the last. And it wasn't just them. In the fields on each side of the road, dozens and dozens of birds were walking to wherever birds would usually fly. A few did try to fly. They flapped their wings much too slowly and did not get more than three inches off the ground. Then they gave up in disgust.

But if the birds had problems with lift-off, they were not the worst ones off. As evening approached, Jack, Jill and Bo heard a horrible CRASH, then a SCREAM, followed by a MOO. A cow had jumped into the moon.

On the other side of a hill, they found an excited crowd gathered at the scene of the accident. The moon had just risen above the horizon and was looking very large as it usually does at the beginning of its shift. The moon is by far the happiest and most easy-going of all who live in Jack's kingdom. However, the moon does have a dark side, and judging by her expression, she was currently showing it.

"She was coming right at me like some maniac!" the moon complained to King Jack. "What kind of crazy animal does such a thing?"

It appeared to Jack that the moon had a black eye from the collision. Then

again, it might only have been a crater.

The cow was certainly injured. She was holding a bag of ice to her nose. "I don't understand it, your Majesty. I've always managed to get enough height before."

"It's true," added a cat who was holding a fiddle. "She usually does make it over the moon."

"That's not the point! Why is she jumping over me, anyway?" screamed the moon as she rose higher into the night sky. "Don't you have a life? Don't you have to get milked or something?" The moon continued complaining and continued rising. Eventually, she was too far away to be heard. The last thing anyone on the ground could make out was the moon shrieking, "I'll be back! I'll be back!"

Jack felt that a kingly speech would be appropriate at this moment. "Good citizens, let us stay calm. Things are not quite right in our land. We must all try to keep our sense of humor."

"I find nothing funny about this situation at all," remarked a dour little dog who happened to be passing by.

"Tell me about it!" said a very large and shiny metal spoon. "I fell from the sky when the giant's castle was pulled down. I've been trying to run away from this place since this morning and I can't budge an inch! It's like some magnet is keeping me stuck to this place."

Jack turned to Jill and Bo Peep. "Would you say we're on the right track?"

"I would say we're definitely getting warmer, Jack," Jill agreed.

"Hmmmm," mused Jack as he remembered the note in the boat, "getting warmer . . ."

"And it's getting dark," Bo Peep pointed out. "We won't have any light to see with."

Suddenly, there was HOWL, then another HOWL, followed by . . . well, another HOWL. Nimble Jack did not manage to jump over his candlestick.

He did manage to burn the seat of his pajamas. And this hurt. Quite a lot by the sounds of it. Jack, Jill and Bo Peep ran in the direction of the howls.

"Ouch!" screamed Nimble Jack once more as he held his rump and hopped around in a manner that could be easily mistaken for a bizarre dance.

"Nimble Jack, are you all right?" asked King Jack.

"Actually, no, Clumsy Jack . . . I mean, your Majesty. I don't understand it. I've always been able to clear the flame before. This is a truly humbling experience."

"I'm so sorry to hear that," said King Jack, not really meaning it.

Allow me to explain. King Jack had spent all his years at school having to put up with the show-off, Nimble Jack. What was worse was he had to tolerate having Nimble Jack tease him about his own lack of athletic ability. It was most likely Nimble Jack who was responsible for giving King Jack the nickname Clumsy Jack. So, although it was not polite or generous, secretly, King Jack did get some delight in Nimble Jack's embarrassment.

"I have jumped over much larger flames than this!" boasted Nimble Jack. "I have jumped over campfires. I have jumped over lava-flowing volcano tops. I have even jumped over my grandfather's birthday cake when he turned ninety-four. Yet here I am unable to even jump over a measly, puny candlestick. I could see someone awkward like you, King Jack, botching it up, but never someone as nimble and quick as I."

"At least my brother has the sense not to jump over burning objects in the first place," scoffed Princess Jill. "Next time, why don't you consider jumping over hurdles, like normal people?"

"Jill," whispered King Jack. "I am touched by your words."

"Nimble Jack is a puffed-up muffin-head. If anyone should get to call you 'clumsy,' it will be me," Jill whispered back.

Jack gave an uncertain smile. "Thank you sister, I think."

"Mr. Nimble," Bo Peep interrupted. "Did you by any chance come across a large flock of sheep lately?"

"I saw a flock down by Pumpkin Eater's place just today. I jumped over a few of them myself."

"Oh, my!" exclaimed Bo Peep. "You didn't jump over them because they were on fire, did you?"

"No, no, I was just trying to get past them. They were blocking the road."

"Your flock of sheep may still be at Pumpkin Eater's place, where we are only now heading towards," gushed King Jack happily to Bo Peep. "Our fates are intertwined, my lady. It was meant to be."

"Oh, how romantic!" sighed Bo Peep.

"Anyway!" shouted Jill before an icky silence had even a chance of showing up. "We need to borrow your candlestick, Nimble Jack, so we can find our way in the darkness. I don't suppose that should be a problem, should it?"

Nimble Jack, who was still rubbing his burned bottom, lowered his head in shame.

"No, I don't think I'll be using it for the time being. But wait, I nearly forgot! Someone came by earlier and left that lantern."

Jill looked at the lantern sitting on the top of a fence post. It was an odd-looking thing with a handle shaped almost like a weather vane. It had an arrow, which was pointing in the direction that the three of them were heading, and instead of a rooster, it had a chicken wearing a crown. Even though he wasn't sure why, Jack felt insulted by the lantern.

"He said it was going to be a dark night," Nimble Jack continued, "and that I should give it to any strangers who should be in need. I suppose you might as well have it."

"Did you see what this man looked like?" asked King Jack.

"Didn't really pay attention," replied Nimble Jack, who would rather gaze at his own reflection anyway. "He kind of looked familiar, but I couldn't describe him for the life of me."

Jill held the lantern before her and continued down the dark road towards Peter Pumpkin Eater's place. King Jack and Bo Peep stayed close behind.

Chapter Eight

For the most part, everyone in King Jack's land got along together. Some were more annoying than others, like Nimble Jack or Reginald, the castle butler, but no one was really avoided at all costs. However, one person came very close, and that was Peter Pumpkin Eater.

It wasn't as if Mr. Pumpkin Eater tried to be more sociable. He wasn't very friendly. He wasn't very trustful.

He wasn't really interested in anyone else's life. Oh, and one other thing: he was totally obsessed with pumpkins. He lived and breathed pumpkins. He had a house made from the shell of a pumpkin. The walls of his house were covered with pictures of pumpkins. As you probably guessed by his name, he ate pumpkins too. There was even a Mrs. Pumpkin Eater who shared his pumpkin-rich life.

Presently, Peter Pumpkin Eater was sitting in his pumpkin patch, waxing and polishing his latest crop of pumpkins. "Ooooh, aren't you a lovely one?" he cooed to a tiny pumpkin held daintily in his palm. "One day, you'll grow up to be a big handsome pumpkin. You'll grow taller than a fence post and plumper than a rain barrel. I'll be so proud of you. I'll show you off to all the other pumpkin growers. And after you grow the biggest you possibly can . . . I'm going to eat you! I'm going to eat you for breakfast and eat you for lunch and eat you for dinner and eat you for a bedtime snack. I'm going to cook you and bake you and fry you and roast you. I'm going to turn you into soup and turn you into pudding. I'm going to eat every little bit of you and I'm going to like it."

"Hello Peter," said Jack. "I hope we're not disturbing anything too important."

"Or too weird," added Jill, under her breath.

"What? Who goes there?" Peter Pumpkin Eater leapt to his feet and squinted into the darkness. "Come out and show yourself, you thieving, pumpkin stealer!"

"It's just me, King Jack. I'm here with my sister Jill and Miss Bo Peep."

Jill brought the lantern closer so that Peter Pumpkin Eater could have a better look at them. They all smiled and tried to look as if they were anything but thieving pumpkin stealers, which they weren't anyway. Peter Pumpkin Eater studied them for a minute and when he was certain they hadn't come to take one of his beloved pumpkins, he relaxed a bit.

"Er . . . sorry, your Majesty. Heard someone lurking about earlier on. Thought he might have come back. So then . . . what can I do for you?"

"We've come to investigate all the strange things that have been happening around your area today," said Jack.

Peter Pumpkin Eater looked puzzled. "Excuse me? What strange things?"

"Surely you noticed all the birds and bugs falling around you," stated Jill.

Peter Pumpkin Eater scratched his balding head. "No, can't say that I have. Of course, I've been awfully busy with my pumpkins, what with watering them, grooming them and reading to them."

"Then did you happen to notice a rather large flock of sheep?" asked Bo Peep sweetly. "I was told that they were near here."

"Oh, sheep I've seen! I was rightly

angry with them too. I had to chase the monsters away because they were nibbling on my beautiful pumpkins."

"To where did you chase this good woman's sheep?" demanded Jack in a stern voice.

"Just onto the road, your Majesty," replied Peter Pumpkin Eater. "Then that darn Nimble Jack caused a ruckus and they all got spooked and ran into my pumpkin house with my wife."

Bo Peep looked at Peter Pumpkin Eater's pumpkin house. It may have looked warm and cozy, as far as one can *be* cozy in a pumpkin shell, but it definitely didn't look big. "I have over two hundred sheep, Mr. Pumpkin Eater. Are you sure they all went into your house?"

"Oh yes. I saw if with my own eyes. They're probably still in there now because I haven't seen them since."

"Would you mind if we have a look then?" asked Jill.

"Help yourself. But mind you don't touch any of my pumpkin magazines!

And tell my wife that I would like some pumpkin sandwiches after I finish up with the polishing."

"I will do no such thing," replied Jill as she went to the door with the others.

It was perfectly clear one second after they peeked in that neither the sheep or Mrs. Pumpkin Eater was still in the house. But two seconds after they peeked in, they discovered a possible reason why. There was a hole in the middle of the pumpkin house floor and stairs running down from it.

"Peter, what do you have in your basement?" asked Jack from one of the windows.

"I don't have anything in my basement," replied Peter Pumpkin Eater, "because I don't have a basement!"

"Well, you have a basement now. What you don't have is a Mrs. Pumpkin Eater."

"Jack, come over here!" Bo Peep called frantically. "Listen!"

Jack came over to the basement entrance and leaned over to listen. There was nothing to hear and he was about to say as much, when just then, he heard a distant *baaaa*.

"I found them!" exclaimed Bo Peep happily. "They are all down there."

But what exactly *is* down there? thought Jack and Jill.

Chapter Nine

The spiral staircase leading from Peter Pumpkin Eater's house went down, down and down. Jack and Jill and Bo Peep had no idea how far underground they were going, and they didn't know what might greet them around each turn. Jack's active imagination did give him a few suggestions though. Giant killer earthworms was one image he was trying desperately to put out of his mind.

Must be brave. Must be brave, Jack thought to himself over and over.

All they had was the light from the lantern and the "baaa" of Bo Peep's sheep to guide them. But when at last they did reach the bottom, they were presented with a most peculiar sight. Before them was a long, metal passageway and it was lit by a string of glass pears, each giving off a strong glow. They couldn't even see the end of the corridor, for it continued on so far into the distance. However, with all these odd lights, Jill decided to turn out the lantern for the time being.

Valiant King Jack fearlessly pushed forward down the strange tunnel without a jot of concern for his own safety. Or to be truly honest, Jack was becoming so scared, he couldn't even make his brain tell his feet to stop walking. He was leading the group only because the tunnel was too narrow to change positions.

But as much as Jack wanted to

be pulling up the rear, Jill wanted to be up front to discover what this underground hideaway was all about. If there was to be an adventure, she sure didn't want to miss it. What Jill really wished was that she had her sword or crossbow or even her sling shot. Jill had been in such a big hurry to catch up with her brother after the luncheon that she didn't even think of bringing anything. If something dangerous were ahead, it would be up to her to protect everyone. Certainly Jack wouldn't be able to, and Jill had even less confidence in icky Bo Peep. Jill sighed and tried to contain her frustration with Jack's slow progress. She wished he would let her get in front and lead the way.

And Bo Peep just wanted to get up front so she could find her poor sheep. Their bleating sounded louder and louder as the three of them inched forward.

"Do you think we might pick up the pace a bit, Jack?" asked Jill impatiently.

"I have to agree with your sister," Bo Peep added. "I think a snail just passed us."

But Jack didn't hear either of them because he was too busy doing what he always did when he was scared: counting Jacks. For some reason, in King Jack's kingdom, Jack is a very popular name. There are a lot of Jacks yet each one is quite different. You can spend a great deal of time trying to remember all of them. And this can be calming because while you're doing that, you don't have to think about the fact that you are walking towards the gaping mouths of giant earthworms.

In his head, King Jack was going over all the Jacks that were in his class at school. "Jack Horner, Jack Spratt, Nimble Jack and Cracker Jack, The Jack of Hearts, The Jack of Spades, not to mention Jack of all Trades. But wait a second . . . "

"What's the matter?" asked Jill. "Why did you stop?"

"I was just thinking. There was a Jack in my class, I'm sure of it."

"Brother, everyone in your class is called Jack."

"Yes, I know. But I can remember every one of them. I can't for the life of me remember this Jack. I can't imagine him or describe him. He's . . . he's unremarkable."

"This is all very fascinating," Bo Peep interrupted, "but could we continue walking, please? We are in a very tight space, very far under the ground."

"Could be worse," replied Jill. "We could be in total darkness without a clue to who or what is around us."

And it was just at that moment that all the pear-shaped lights went out, leaving Jack and Jill and Bo Peep in total darkness without a clue to who or what was around them. "You're quite right, sister," Jack's shaky voice said in the blackness. "This is indeed worse. Ahhhhhhhhhhh!"

Now, if Jack had the ability to see

in total darkness, he would have seen his sister roll her eyes in disgust at him. Jill thought Jack was screaming like a baby because he was so frightened. Jack *was* frightened, it's true, but that wasn't why he was screaming. If Jill had the ability to see in total darkness, she would have seen the floor open up beneath Jack's feet, and Jack suddenly falling down a shaft. *That* was why Jack was screaming. But neither brother nor sister nor even Bo Peep had the ability to see in total darkness. That was why Jill and Bo Peep soon began screaming too, as they fell down the same shaft.

"Ahhhhhhhhhhhhhhhh!"

Even as they screamed, none of them could help but notice how long they were sliding down the shaft. Twisting and turning, Jack, Jill and Bo Peep fell for many seconds. It is well-known that screaming will continue for as long as one has the breath to keep on screaming. Or until something better comes along. In this case, what did come along was pain. The shaft ended at a hole in a wall. One by one, all three of them were propelled out of the hole onto a hard, cement floor. Their "Ahhhhhhs!" quickly turned into "Owwwws!"

Jack, who was the first to slide down the shaft, the first to land with a thud and the first to recover from the pain in his bottom, was now the first to take in the surroundings. "Oh, my," said Jack, which doesn't really tell you a whole bunch. But consider that his jaw fell open and his eyes widened to the size of one of his mother's fine china plates, and perhaps then you will be prepared to understand what he saw.

First of all, they were in jail. The hole emptied them into a small cave with bars along one side. There was another jail cell, exactly the same, next to them. It contained an older woman who looked extremely, *extremely* happy. This was quite odd considering she was, after all, sitting in a jail cell. Jack knew

her to be Mrs. Pumpkin Eater. On the other side of her was yet another jail cell, also exactly the same, except for the over two hundred sheep lounging about inside it. All three jails connected off of a humongous cavern. In the middle of the humongous cavern was an equally humongous machine. In the middle of this machine was a humongous U-shaped object pointing upwards. On the far side of the humongous U-shaped object was a normal sized man. Jack couldn't tell who he was because his face was hidden in the shadows.

"Hello Jack," the mysterious man said in a low voice. "I'm so glad you could drop in. And right on time."

Chapter Ten

Jack and Jill and Bo Peep peered into the darkness. They were hoping to get a better look at this mysterious person, but he seemed to be in no hurry to show himself.

"What did you mean by 'right on time'?" asked Jack. "How did you know we would come here?"

"Because I went to a lot of effort to make sure you would find your way here," replied the voice. "And *not* find your way back."

"So you left the lantern with Nimble Jack?" asked Jill.

"Getting warmer," said the voice, obviously enjoying this moment.

"Getting warmer," repeated Jack. "The boat! And the map! You wanted me to find the map?"

"Oh yes. I wasn't taking any chances that you would screw up and get lost."

"Then I suppose you were the wolf too?" Bo Peep joined in.

"Guilty as charged," replied the voice, and then added slowly, "Ha, ha, ha."

"The hedge! *You* pruned the hedge near the hill we fell down!" accused Jill, who didn't like being the butt of anyone's joke.

"Not to mention getting you in trouble with the old lady in the park."

"And the one who told Reginald I was a big chicken," added Jack.

"Oh yes, but that was just my way of having some fun," said the voice that was sounding less amused and more frightening.

Enough was enough. If King Jack was supposed to be scared of this person, he might as well find out who this person was.

"Who *are* you?" he demanded.

"I am Jack," replied the voice from the shadows.

"Jack? Jack who? You're not Jack Frost or Jack-in-the-Pulpit? But you do sound familiar."

"Just . . . plain . . . Jack," insisted the voice.

"Well, I've never heard of you," sneered Jill.

"Of course you haven't heard of me! How could you? Every Jack in the kingdom has some kind of description. That is, except for me. How would anyone tell me apart from a Tom, Dick or Harry?"

"That shouldn't be too hard," replied King Jack helpfully. "Tom is Tom Thumb. Dick is Little Dickie and Harry is Hairy Harry, on account of his back.

No one would mistake you with any of them, I should imagine."

"Stop it! Stop rubbing it in!" screamed the voice so loudly that even the sheep became interested. "But no, they wouldn't mistake me for anyone, would they? No thanks to you!" In a blink, the voice in the shadows became a body rushing towards the jail cell. He revealed himself to be a boy of about the same age as King Jack. Up close, with his face pressed against the bars, this boy appeared . . . well, I'm sorry to say, unremarkable. He was not nearly as scary as everyone had imagined. Plain, average face. Nose not too big and not too small. Eyes just the right distance apart. There was nothing really notable about him except for just one detail: he looked very very angry. "You ruined my name, Clumsy King Jack," he hissed.

"Me? What do I have to do with it?" King Jack was quite taken by surprise.

"If it wasn't for you being such a

nice guy, I'd have had a great name! *You* should have been plain Jack, not me. I should have been Naughty Jack or Impish Jack. But instead, you turned into Clumsy Jack, and no one even notices me!"

King Jack was no longer surprised. Now he was confused. "But everyone at school called me Clumsy Jack because I kept falling down stairs and walking into doors."

"Ha! You never fell. I tripped you! I pushed open the doors so you would walk into them! I was always standing right there, waiting to get blamed, waiting for someone to see me and say, 'Naughty Jack! Bad Jack!' And they would have if you didn't keep saying, 'Sorry, I must have slipped, sorry, I didn't see that rope strung across the floor, sorry, my fault, sorry.' Oooooh, you made me so mad!"

King Jack was no longer confused. Now he moved on to being astonished. "You mean I wasn't really clumsy at first?"

"No, King Jack, you weren't. But because you were so willing to blame yourself instead of me, I had to end up staying the same — just plain Jack."

"Why don't we call you Just Plain Jack then?" suggested Jill, who was not very good at making suggestions.

"Just Plain Jack? Do you think that's going to make me feel better? Why don't I just call myself Average Jack, or So-so Jack or Fill-in-the-blank Jack?"

"Well, I suppose those are all good names too," replied King Jack, trying much too hard to be encouraging.

"No, they're not! They're boring! Boring! But after I finish destroying your kingdom, I will have a truly interesting name. I will be known as . . . Evil Jack."

"Oh," said King Jack and Princess Jill together.

"That's all very well and good," said Bo Peep, who didn't care for dramatic pauses, "but what do my poor little sheep have to do with your silly plans?"

"Absolutely nothing, anymore," replied the soon-to-be-evil Jack. "I just needed them to help lure King Jack here."

"Then why must they be locked up?" demanded Bo Peep.

"Because they eat everything! They're worse than goats! They would eat my evil machine if they had half a chance."

"My poor babies," Bo Peep lamented as she stared at the cage full of sheep. "It's not their fault that they have such healthy appetites. Some of them are growing, like Little Sammy and Frankie and Dean and . . ."

"Speaking about evil machines," remarked Jill, quickly changing the subject, "I couldn't help notice how much like a big magnet that U-shaped thing over there is."

"That's because it is a big magnet," replied the evil-in-the-making Jack, "but not just any kind of magnet. It doesn't just attract metal. This magnet can be programmed to attract anything I choose."

"Eggs?" asked King Jack.

"Yes."

"Cradles?" asked Princess Jill.

"Yes."

"Bridges?" asked Bo Peep.

"Husha, husha, we all fall down," replied so-close-to-sounding-evil Jack. "As you may have noticed, I can set it on insect, bird or cow as well. Are you not impressed?"

"I suppose," yawned King Jack, "if you're into that kind of thing."

Practically-evil Jack was practically furious. "What do you mean, 'you suppose'? Were you not impressed with my motorboat or the electricity that gave light to the tunnel you walked along? Have you ever seen such amazing inventions in all your kingdom?"

"Look, Evilish-kind-of Jack. I live in a kingdom where chickens talk, families live in huge shoes, giants live in castles in the sky, pigs build houses and bears eat porridge. There really isn't too much more that could amaze me."

"Fine! Well, soon, nothing at all will amaze you. In half an hour it will be midnight. At the strike of twelve, after a few more calculations involving math skills far more superior than you could ever comprehend, I will set my super magnet to attract . . . everything. Do you know what will happen then?"

King Jack and Princess Jill and Bo Peep shook their heads.

"NOTHING! Nothing will happen! Zilch! No one in the kingdom will be able to move an inch. No flying cows. No wall-sitting eggs. No water-fetching Jacks. You will all be frozen in your tracks. You will all be . . . boring. You will all be just plain, like I was."

Evil Jack, who as far as King Jack, his sister and Bo Peep were now concerned, was indeed evil, left the cavern while laughing a very sinister laugh. "One half hour!" he shouted as the door bolted shut behind him.

Chapter Eleven

For two solid minutes after Evil Jack left them, King Jack, Princess Jill and Bo Peep didn't say a word. To be fair, what can you say of any importance after someone tells you they intend to turn everyone you know into living statues? However, after two minutes, King Jack thought of something worth mentioning.

"We really should try to stop him."

"But we're in jail, Jack," countered Jill. "There's not a whole lot we can do in our position."

"Don't worry, Jill, something will come . . ."

"Don't you dare say it, Jack! Nothing is going to come up! Not this time. Uh-uh. You can stare at clouds all you want, but you won't find any silver linings. This is one time where we won't be living happily after. I hate this! I hate this! I hate this!"

"Well, you did insist on having an adventure."

"That's not fair!" yelled Jill at her brother.

"And you did insist that I could depend on your skills in times like this."

"Double not fair!"

"Excuse me!" shouted Bo Peep, sounding slightly annoyed. "I don't want to interrupt your little brother and sister spat, but I do think we are running out of time. I would like to make a suggestion, if I may."

Jack and Jill looked slightly embarrassed and lowered their heads. "Yes, you are quite right, Bo," said Jack. "What was your plan?"

"I thought that maybe we could use this," Bo Peep explained as she rummaged through her frilly handbag and pulled out a small object for them to see. It was about the size of a pencil with a hook at the end.

"What? A candy cane?" said Jill.

"No, it's not a candy cane. It's a shepherd's crook. I use it to keep my sheep in line."

"I could see how that might be useful," said Jill doubtfully, "if your sheep were three inches tall!"

"What I think my sister is saying in her usual tactful way is, what use can such a small object have in getting us out of jail?"

Bo Peep was completely annoyed now. Just because she was sweet didn't mean she was stupid. If it wasn't for the fact that she too was in jail with

Jack and Jill, she would have half a mind to leave them where they were for a while.

"Well, my plan was to take the 'candy cane' and stretch it out to its normal size like I do when I don't require it to be small enough to fit into my hand-bag." And that is what Bo Peep did. She pulled out the shepherd's crook until it opened up to eight feet in length. "Then, my plan was to reach out and use my 'candy cane' to snag the set of jail keys that are hanging over there." And this too is what she did. For their part, Jack and Jill just continued looking more embarrassed.

Unfortunately, the key ring didn't come off the hook as smoothly as they had wished, and rather than staying on Bo Peep's crook, it got catapulted through the air and landed just in front of Mrs. Pumpkin Eater's prison cell.

"That's not a problem," said Jack encouragingly. "Mrs. Pumpkin Eater, would you be so kind as to use the keys to let yourself out and then let us out as well?"

Mrs. Pumpkin Eater, who hadn't said a word the whole time, looked over towards Jack and said very happily, "Nope."

"Are you out of your mind?" screamed Jill tactfully. "We have only a few minutes to escape and save ourselves from doom! Don't you want to escape?"

"Not particularly," replied Mrs. Pumpkin Eater.

"But, why not?" asked King Jack.

"I live with a man who thinks of nothing else other than pumpkins! I thought it was kind of cute when we first got married, but now it's been twenty years! I don't want to look at another pumpkin, taste another pumpkin or smell another pumpkin again! I'm quite happy right where I am, thank you very much."

"This isn't good," said King Jack, stating the obvious.

"Evil Jack will be here any second," moaned Jill.

"Dear Mrs. Pump- dear kind lady," Bo Peep said, correcting herself. "I can understand that you don't want to let yourself escape, but the door to the prison where my sheep are being kept is within your reach. Could you find it in your heart to let them enjoy their last few minutes of freedom?"

Mrs. Pump- I mean, the dear, kind lady thought about it for a moment and then got up and grabbed the keys in front of her cell. "I don't have anything against sheep." She reached through the bars and stuck a key into the lock of the sheep's prison door. It clicked open.

"Oh, well, that's all fine then," said Jill, not really meaning it. "As long as the sheep are happy."

Suddenly, there was a large bang as Evil Jack slammed open the door into the cavern.

Looking quite pleased with himself, he walked over to King Jack and thrust his pocket watch through the bars and into the king's face. The two hands were facing twelve. "It's Show Time!" Turning on his heel, he strode to his evil machine and sat himself down at the control panel.

Bo Peep leaned over to King Jack and whispered, "I've told you a lot of my sheep's names, haven't I?"

"As much as I do enjoy listening about your sheep, Bo, I'm afraid this isn't probably the best time to resume that conversation."

"But I haven't told you all their names," she continued. "I haven't told you about Spike."

Even Jill had to turn to Bo Peep at hearing that. "You have a sheep called Spike?"

"Isn't that a rather odd name for a sheep?" added King Jack.

"Spike isn't your usual *kind* of sheep."

"Quiet over there!" shouted Evil Jack from his controls. "I have put the final program instructions into my super-magnet. I am now ready to make history."

Evil Jack got up from his chair and

moved towards the base of the super-magnet. He put his hand on a large red lever and turned towards his prisoners. "Behold! From this moment on, I will no longer be known to the world as just plain Jack. I will be known forevermore as . . . "

"Spike!" shouted Bo Peep.

"Spike?" repeated Evil Jack. "No, no, no. Haven't you been paying attention. My name is going to be . . . "

"Spike! Attack!" yelled Bo Peep towards the jail cell piled full of sheep. There was a rustling of wool, then a few "baaas," and then suddenly, the unlocked cell door swung open, and out sprang the meanest looking sheep you'd ever want to meet on a lonely dark night. Jack and Jill both instantly gasped in shock. Evil Jack instantly realized that up until then, when he had considered that Bo Peep's troublesome sheep were capable of eating anything, he hadn't yet considered that might also include himself.

Spike turned ominously towards Evil Jack and growled. He trampled the ground like a bull. He lowered his terrifying head and came after Evil Jack in a fast charge. With one giant leap, Spike landed straight on top of Evil Jack, pushing him away from the super-magnet and keeping him undeniably pinned down for good. Meanwhile, another sheep by the name of Buttercup grabbed the key ring in her mouth and took it over to Bo Peep, with her tail wagging behind her.

"Good Spike. Good Buttercup," said Bo Peep as she unlocked her own cell. "Bad Evil Jack," she threw in, just for good measure.

Jack and Jill were still visibly impressed with Bo Peep and how she handled the situation. After having worried and fretted about how *they* would save the day, neither brother nor sister seriously considered someone else might be better suited to the task. Bo Peep was truly liking all this new attention.

"Wow," Jill managed to say. "Really . . . wow."

"You have saved the kingdom, my lady," said King Jack, bowing before her. "You must come with all your sheep to the castle where we will hold a large banquet in your honor."

"But what shall we do with him," asked Bo Peep, referring to the boy with a growling sheep standing on his chest.

"We'll take it from here." It was Sir Humpty Dumpty, held together with duct tape but looking no worse for wear. He was accompanied by a brigade of guards who wasted no time taking Evil Jack in hand.

"Sir Dumpty, what on earth or under earth are you doing here?"

"Your mother sent us, your Majesty. Long story short, we followed your trail to the river, built a new bridge, crossed over the bridge, followed your trail some more, avoided Peter Pumpkin Eater and then found the entrance and finally, the tunnel."

"Why didn't you fall down the shaft into one of the jail cells like we did?" asked Jill.

"Well, we would have, but I couldn't quite fit through it, which therefore allowed us to reach the elevator-thingy on the far side instead. Now, are all of you all right?"

"Yes, Sir Humpty. Thank you," said Jack.

"I don't mind saying that it was reckless of the two of you to go off on your own. Your father entrusted you into my care. A king should show better judgement, Jack. And Jill? If you ever intend to join the Royal Guard, which I hope you will, you'd better stop rushing blindly into trouble. You did well, and I'm proud of you both, but I was terribly worried just the same."

"We didn't do anything," said Jill. "It was Bo who saved the kingdom."

"Then a hearty thank you to you, Miss," said Sir Humpty courteously to

Bo Peep. "Now, shall I take this scoundrel away?"

"Please do," insisted Jill.

"All right then. Come on Jack!" ordered Humpty Dumpty.

"Sir Humpty, to avoid any confusion in the future, this fellow is henceforth to be referred to as Evil Jack."

"If you say so, your Majesty."

"Do you mean it?" asked Evil Jack in disbelief. "I can keep my name?"

"You certainly deserve it," replied King Jack.

"Thank you, your Highness! Did you hear, everyone? I'm Evil Jack. EVIL JACK! Oooh, I like the ring of that."

"I didn't mean it as a compliment," scolded King Jack. "If you intend to stay in this kingdom, you will have to change your ways."

"Yes, your Majesty," said Evil Jack, not really meaning it.

"Then we'll find you a less dangerous name. Something upbeat. Something 'nice.'"

Suddenly, Evil Jack didn't look quite so happy as he was being dragged away by the guards.

Everyone eventually returned to the surface, including Mrs. Pumpkin Eater, who intended to have a long talk with her husband. King Jack and his sister Princess Jill and Miss Bo Peep and two hundred sheep made their way back to the castle, guided by the torch light of Sir Dumpty's men before them.

"I have to say, Jack," said Jill to her brother, "this was not the kind of adventure I was hoping for. I admit, I was quite worried back then. Things could have ended badly, don't you think?"

"Oh, I don't know," said Jack as he looked over to Bo Peep. "Something usually comes up. It always does."

This time, Jill didn't mind so much the icky silence that followed them the rest of the way back home.

One day Dan Bar-el noticed just how many things and people fall to the ground in children's stories and nursery rhymes. In *Things are Looking Up, Jack*, he explains all that falling and puts a stop to it once and for all. Brave and creative in life as well as in his writing, Dan once met a grizzly bear atop a mountain in Jasper National Park and survived to tell the tale by entertaining it with his harmonica. A preschool teacher, Dan lives and writes in Vancouver, British Columbia.

For a complete catalog and information on the free teachers' guides that are available for many of Orca Book Publishers' books, please call 1-800-210-5277 or visit www.orcabook.com.